Billy, an Owl, and a Bear

Lost and Alone

by

T.D. Roth

T.D. Roth

Copyright © 2023 T.D. Roth
All rights reserved.
ISBN: 978-1-9991125-8-5

Cover: Compilation from Pixaby

DEDICATION

To all young boys and girls with a love of outdoor adventure, animals, and friendship.

CONTENTS

CHAPTER 1	3
CHAPTER 2	7
CHAPTER 3	15
CHAPTER 4	19
CHAPTER 5	21
CHAPTER 6	33
CHAPTER 7	43
CHAPTER 8	53
CHAPTER 9	59
CHAPTER 10	65
CHAPTER 11	71
CHAPTER 12	77
CHAPTER 13	83
CHAPTER 14	89
CHAPTER 15	99
CHAPTER 16	107

ACKNOWLEDGMENTS

Credit must be given to my mother and father. Dad took me with him to stream and mountain long before I could handle a rod or rifle. Mom was a reader and instilled in me a love of books. I still enjoy a good read every night before going to sleep. Now my parents live on in many of the words I put to paper.

CHAPTER 1

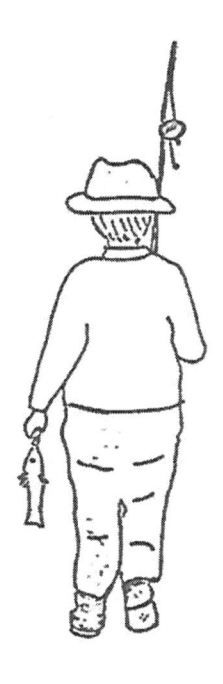

I LOVE FISHING. Trout, perch, bass, catfish, river, lake, creek, ocean. I love fishing. That's how I first met my best friend, Tommy Little Bear. It was at a rocky outcrop along the Chino River where it flows from Lake Vatea. During the spring and summer it's a great place for trout and whitefish. In the late summer, chinook, pink, and sockeye salmon thrash their way to the spawning grounds. The sockeye were running that fall and a dozen or more fishermen lined the bank where I normally fish–too crowded for me. So I crossed the bridge upriver from the fishing beach and rode my bicycle about a mile along the railroad tracks to a trailhead where a rope dangles down a steep path leading to the river. At the base of the path, a gravelly beach lies to the right of a rocky bluff. I hiked to the left across small, oval boulders and large rocks to a spot just above a small waterfall. Not many people fish that spot, and for good reason. My first time there I lost at least a half a dozen hooks and sinkers on the rocky bottom before finding what I call the "sweet spot." This particular Saturday morning there was no sign of life; no occasional fish leaping up the rapids; no murky forms streaking across the bottom; and definitely no action as I cast again and again into the swift current.

When a long, dark shadow darkened the rocks beside me, my pulse quickened, and my stomach tightened. My immediate thought was *bear*! Bears were salmon fishing long before people came along, and they don't appreciate twelve-year-old boys invading their territory. My first impulse was to run but you'll never outrun a bear. Climbing a tree doesn't work either. We had one climb the tree behind our house to help himself to the birdfeeder. Besides, whatever stood behind me was blocking the trail. I slowly turned to face a boy who, despite casting a huge shadow, was about my size. He had dark skin and long black hair.

"H-hello, I said. "Are you fishing?"

He nodded.

"W-well, where's your pole?"

"I don't need one," he replied, breaking into a wide smile. "You won't catch any fish here today. My family has nets on the other side of the bluff. Come with me and I will show you how *my* people catch fish."

I let out my breath and smiled. It seems there's an instant connection between young boys, especially when it comes to fishing. I had heard about First Nations people netting salmon and couldn't pass up a chance to see how they did it. I quickly picked up my gear and followed him down the trail.

"My name's Billy," I said. "And yours?"

"Tommy. Tommy Little Bear."

"That's a funny name. Why Little Bear?"

"A mother bear and her cub passed through our garden the day I was born. My father saw it as a sign and named me Little Bear. My friends just call me Tommy."

CHAPTER 2

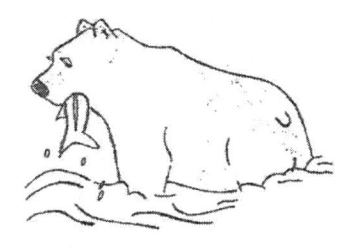

WHEN WE ROUNDED the bluff, I saw a net that had been strung halfway across the river. A woman tended a kettle of tea which hung from a tripod of willow limbs over a large fire. An older man and woman sat on a big log, each cradling a tin cup between their hands. Two little girls laughed and giggled as they waded and splashed in the shallow water along the beach. A large, brown retriever let out a yelp and bounded toward us.

"He won't bite," said Tommy. "He's glad to see us. Hold out your hand so he can get your scent." The dog jumped up and placed its paws on my chest. "Down Jasper! That's no way to treat my friend. Get down!" Jasper leapt, circled us, and ran back to bark at fish that were trapped in a holding pool. "He's just a puppy but will soon become a protector of our family. You should have a dog. Then I couldn't sneak up on you. Come, I will take you to my grandfather."

Tommy's grandpa wore an olive-green cap, a red plaid shirt, and tattered bib overalls. Apart from two long grey braids, he didn't look that different from my own grandpa. The older woman was dressed in a similar shirt and blue jeans. Her hair, light grey with occasional streaks of dark brown, was set in one long braid which trailed down her back and sported a lone dark feather. Both wore calf-high rubber boots.

"Grandfather," said Tommy. "I have a new friend. This is Billy. He was fishing on the other side of the bluff. I told him he should wait until we pull our nets."

The old man smiled. "Welcome to our family." He pointed to a large rock. "Sit. You must join us in some bannock and tea. We will soon pull the nets. Perhaps you can help."

"Glad to meet you, Mr.–"

"Sorry," interrupted Tommy. My Grandfather is Chief Jesse Dubois."

"–er, Chief Jesse. I'll be happy to help."

The younger woman brought cups of hot tea for me and Tommy.

"This is my mother," said Tommy.

"Glad to meet you, Mrs. Bear."

She looked at Tommy, laughed, and shook her head. "Tommy, Tommy, Tommy. You're *our* Little Bear." Then she turned to me, "Our family name is Dubois. And I'm glad to meet you too. Now I have to get back to the fire. Tommy's father and uncle will arrive soon. I must have a good stew ready for them."

I envied Tommy. My family consisted of my mom and little sister. I rarely saw my grandpa and had never met my dad. I imagined myself as Tommy's cousin or brother. "Billy Dubois" had a nice ring to it.

Tommy bumped my shoulder. "Look, the nets are filling with fish. See how the netting curves in the water. When father returns we will pull them and place the catch in the holding pool. Come with me. We must place more rocks around the pool to keep the salmon from escaping back to the river."

We were soon sweating in the late morning sun as we built up the sides of the pool. The water seeping into the pool would keep dozens of salmon alive and fresh until they were packed in coolers of ice and carried to the trucks parked above.

"Why do you take so many?" I asked. "I'm only allowed two sockeye per day, and your family is taking a truckload. Do you think that's fair?"

"Yes," answered Tommy. "You are taking enough for your family whereas we are fishing for our clan. Our catch will be shared with the *whole* family and must last through the winter. It has always been this way. Just wait. Once our family needs are met, my father will pull the nets. We would never take all the fish. Most must make their way to the spawning grounds so there will be salmon for next year, and the next, and the next. They were entrusted to us by our ancestors and must be cared for."

"Look!" Tommy pointed across the river where a cinnamon bear was wading into a shallow pool opposite the nets. The bruin sat down in the stream and began batting at passing salmon. "He comes every year to join us in the harvest."

Tommy tapped his chest with his right thumb. "We are part of the Bear Clan. I would never hurt or kill a bear. Who knows, this bear might be my great grandfather come to watch over us."

Our conversation ceased as Tommy's father, Albert Dubois, and his Uncle Jimmy descended the hill carrying large coolers of ice. It was time to get to work. Tommy and I were soon pulling salmon from the net and tossing them into the holding pool. Mr. Dubois wielded a short pole with a portion of deer antler attached as a gaff to pull fish from the pond. Once the salmon were packed in ice, the coolers were hauled up the hill to two pickup trucks and the net was pulled to dry. Then we sat around the fire sipping tea and savoring fresh warm bannock. As I slurped the last of my tea, I rose from the fire.

"Thank you, Chief Jesse, for letting me help. I had great fun. My mom expects me home before dark and I need to get going."

The Chief smiled. "Little Bear, get two sockeye for your friend."

"But I didn't think you could give salmon to people outside your family," I said.

"Come closer." Chief Jesse placed a hand on each of my shoulders and peered into my eyes. "Hmm. You have yellow hair and a round pale face, yet your spirit mingles with ours. Your eyes are large and dark like those of the barred owl. Yes, it is the spirit of the owl that I see. He is confident and resourceful and imparts wisdom and strength. I name you Little Owl. You are now part of our family and Little Bear is your brother. As Chief, I give you fish. Take these to your mother. And Little Owl, you come visit soon. Little Bear needs your friendship."

T.D. Roth

CHAPTER 3

AT SCHOOL Tommy and I became inseparable. We attended the same classes, played the same sports, and spent every spare minute together. On the weekends we fished on the river or explored the nearby woods. Tommy began teaching me the hunting skills he had learned from his grandfather. He was more like a brother than a friend.

I was scared the first time I visited Tommy's home. On the reserve my pale skin and yellow hair stood out like a white chicken in a flock of reds. Yet, as Tommy's friend, I was treated no differently than the other children.

Chief Jesse had taught his family to maintain many of the old ways, and Grandmother Dubois insisted on performing a smudge ceremony before I sat to eat my first meal with their family.

"Little Owl," she said. "Sit." She placed an ash-stained abalone shell, a long braid of grass, a small bundle of sage, and a large dark feather on the table. "We must prepare our minds and hearts to enjoy the peace and blessings of the Creator."

A small portion of the braided grass was placed in the shell. "The sweetgrass is the hair of Mother Earth and teaches of her gentleness, love, and kindness. The three strands remind us of the balance we need of mind, body, and spirit." She pinched off a few leaves of sage and added them to the shell. "The sage is to ward off bad spirits. This feather is from an eagle, the most sacred of the birds. As the eagle rises to the heavens, it carries our prayers to the Creator."

Grandmother Dubois lit the offering and wafted the flame with the feather. "You never blow on the flame. We always use the feather to fan the breath of the earth."

Once the mixture began to smolder, the old woman lightly waved the feather over and back in the smoke. "First we must purify the feather." She then rose from the table, carrying the shell while wafting the smoke. "I smudge around the table to rid of any bad spirits in the room and to invite good spirits to join us." She returned to her chair. "Now we will use our hands and palms to fan the smoke over our heads and hair to bring good thoughts. That's it; just do as I do. We draw the smoke to our eyes to remind us to see good in everything; to our mouths that we will speak proper things; and to our hearts that we will have feelings of love and gentleness. Now pull the smoke around your body asking for health and energy." Grandmother Dubois stood, took the shell and feather, and fanned the other parts of the room. Coming back to the table, she set the smoldering shell beside me. "We must let it burn out on its own, Little Owl."

I was reminded of the incense used in our church and the votive candles flickering before the statues of Mary and Joseph. A feeling of peace and purpose filled my heart. I felt that I was part of a real family, and that the Dubois accepted me as one of their very own.

CHAPTER 4

THE SNOW FLEW and the motors roared as Tommy and I sped toward a hunting cabin hidden between the tall peaks of the Mystic Mountains. Because of heavy snow, the old overgrown road could only be found by following a slight indentation in the treetops. We were crossing a clearing when Tommy dropped behind and flagged me ahead. Just before reaching the trees I looked back and saw him disappear behind a terrifying wall of snow and debris. *Avalanche!* I twisted the right handle to full throttle and raced toward the edge of the clearing. Then....

Phew, phew, phew. I gasped for breath. *Phew, phew, phew.* My head hurt and my brain was fuzzy. *Where am I? What happened?* I found myself buried in a deep snow drift with my chest and face lodged against the rough bark of a Douglas fir. My heavy parka had spared me from a broken nose. I slowly moved my arms and legs. The snowmobile lay embedded on its side where it had smashed into a large spruce. One handlebar thrust forth like a drowning man reaching for help. I clawed my way out of a deep tree well and looked back at a sea of boulder-like chunks of ice and snow mixed with the debris of scrub oak from higher up the mountain. There was no Tommy and no hope of finding him. The pass going back was sealed with ice and snow. I was lost and alone. I squatted on my haunches and held my head. *Oh God, what am I going to do? What am I going to do?*

CHAPTER 5

THE SNOWMOBILE was damaged beyond repair. Even if it were operable, it was too heavy to pull from the snow. Knowing that Chief Jesse's cabin would have most of what we needed, Tommy and I had packed light. I dug out a pair of snowshoes, a battered .30-30, and a box of shells that belonged to Chief Jesse. My sleeping bag was torn but not ruined. The food box had disappeared with Tommy. How I wished it had been on my sled. My backpack contained a couple packages of dried salmon and a small bag of bannock flour that Grandmother Dubois had given me as we left. I sat on an old windfall, forlornly looking at my precious few belongings, and wondering what to do and where to go. My only hope was to find the cabin.

"Kroo, krooo. Ank, ank, ank. Krooo." A small owl peered at me from the ragged snag of a blown-down spruce. With its grey-striped plumage it could easily have been mistaken for part of the tree. *"Ank, ank, ank."*

"Hey, little buddy," I said.

It turned its head as though listening, then looked at me and blinked two large brown eyes.

"No wonder people talk about being 'wise as an owl.' You sure have the look."

"Ock, ock, ock. Buhoo." It launched from the stump and flew about twenty yards to the lower limb of a ponderosa pine. The owl swiveled its head toward me and blinked. *"Ock, ock, ock."* Then it glided back to the fallen tree roots and

stared at me with those humongous dark eyes. "*Ank, ank, ank.*"

"If you're looking for something to eat, that makes two of us. And I'll bet your hunting skills are better than mine." The owl danced from foot to foot on its heavily feathered legs. "I like your snow pants. All set for the cold. Guess I look as strange to you as you do to me. Sorry, I can't help you."

The bird turned its head toward the ponderosa pine and flew to the same limb as before. "*Ock, ock, ock. Buhoo.*"

"Are you trying to tell me something?" I secured the snowshoes to my boots and shouldered the pack and rifle. "Appears to me that we're going in the same direction." When I reached the pine, the bird flew to a spruce twenty yards ahead and waited.

It looked at me, "*Ock, ock, ock. Buhoo.*" and flew again. My eyes widened and my mouth dropped. I remembered Chief Jesse saying, "*Your eyes are large and dark like those of the owl. Yes, it is the spirit of the owl that I see."* If the bear was Tommy's spirit animal, could the owl be mine? The bird continued this strange ritual as I followed it through the forest.

As the day shortened, I was led to a clearing alongside the overhang of a steep rock formation. The three essentials for survival are shelter, water, and food–in that order. The rock face and trees provided ample shelter. Snow gave the necessary water. My precious dried salmon would suffice for food. The owl sat on a large boulder and watched while I gathered dry moss, dead twigs, and old limbs for a fire. My matches would have to be used sparingly and the fire would need tending through the night. Once the flames were blazing and my sleeping bag was spread, I took some salmon from my pack. *Just a pinch. How long will this have to last?* The dark crept around me as the owl softly chirred,*"Erk, erk, erk."*

Night was turning dusky grey when I opened my eyes. Venus twinkled farewell on the horizon. Frost clung to the sleeping bag around my mouth and nose. I was hungry and cold. *The fire! I didn't mind the fire.* I flung open the sleeping bag, slipped into my boots, and rushed to the fire pit. A quick poke with a stick uncovered a few fading coals. A handful of moss and twigs soon revived a flame. Within minutes a blazing fire warmed the morning.

"*Kroo, kroo. Ank, ank, ank.*" My feathered friend was perched on the boulder.

"Owl, you came back."

"*Ank, ank, ank.*" A fresh-killed snowshoe rabbit lay at the base of the rock. Owl blinked his eyes and hopped on his feathered legs in a simple bird dance. "*Erk, erk, erk.*"

"Thank you, my friend. Thank you."

Skinning a rabbit is fairly easy, though I have to admit that I had never done it myself. But I had watched Tommy's dad do it with a couple rabbits they raised on their farm. I tied the back legs to an overhanging limb with a lace from one of my boots, then cut through the fur around each leg near the rear paws. After slitting the hide down each leg toward the tail, I was able to peel it off the body by pulling it down and over the front legs and head. The skin was then inside out. It was like pulling off a turtleneck sweater. After removing the guts, I ran a large branch up the inside of the carcass. Within minutes the fresh meat sizzled and crackled over the fire. My twelve years of roasting hotdogs and marshmallows was being put to good use. By the time I took the rabbit from the fire, it was just short of being jerky, which meant that I could save some for later.

"Ock, ock, ock. Buhoo." Owl did his little dance, flew about thirty feet, and returned. It was time to clean up camp and move on. We resumed the ritual of the preceding day–Owl flying ahead and me laboring through two feet of snow on my oversized snowshoes. I was soon soaked in sweat. My legs ached and my lungs hurt. Whenever I stopped to rest, the cold cut through my parka. Maybe I had made a mistake

in following this strange bird. I was about to give up when the trees dwindled away at the edge of an immense mountain meadow. Whoever said that boys never cry, never met this boy. Tears trickled down my face as Owl took to the air and winged toward a line of trees in the distance.

"Wait! Wait," I called. Tommy had told me that the trail followed an ancient road that could be found by looking for a slight dip in the treetops. Owl, now a dot in the sky, disappeared at just such a spot.

The day was passing, the sun was high, and I was spent. The thought of trudging across a mile of deep snow was depressing. I took off my pack and slumped against the trunk of a tree. *Maybe I should set up camp here.* I eyeballed the surrounding trees and brush. There was no natural shelter and no clearing for a fire. I could crawl under the limbs of a large spruce like a wary rabbit hiding from the coyotes, but it would be a long, cold night. If I lit a fire, melting snow would trickle from the limbs above. Then

I'd be cold *and* wet. Maybe the owl wasn't such a trusty guide after all.

A faint *"kroo, krooo,"* drifted across the meadow. *"Ock, ock, ock. Buhoo, buhooo."*

I shouldered my pack and stepped from the trees onto the barren expanse. Then I smiled. *Owl, you knew, didn't you.* The wind and sun had formed a thick crust of ice on the surface of the snow. My boots would have broken through, but the snowshoes gave plenty of support. Mind you, it was still a long trek to the other side. Soon my legs ached. *Left, right, left, right.* I set my lips in grim determination, kept my head down, and shuffled one snowshoe after the other. *Left, right, left, right.* The pack straps cut into my shoulders. *Left, right, left, right.* As the sun neared the horizon, the wind whipped crystals of snow into my face and the temperature plummeted. I stumbled to my knees. *I'm not going to make it. O God, I'm not going to make it.*

"Erk, erk, erk," Owl chirred from the lower limb of a pine only fifteen yards away. *"Erk, erk, erk."* He blinked as if to say, "What took you so long?" Then he swooped into the trees, landed on a dead branch, and danced his little jig. *"Ock, ock, ock."* The branch was a weathered pole that was lashed about four feet off the ground between two trees. Irregular sticks were propped on one side to form a crude shelter. On the open side, a circle of smoke-blackened rocks formed a makeshift fire pit.

I held my hand between the sun and the horizon. Only two fingers separated the sun from the skyline. Tommy had taught me that each finger represents fifteen minutes, which meant that I had thirty minutes before dusk and another fifteen before dark. The first order of business was fresh boughs for the side of the lean-to and a few for bedding.

An hour later I sat before a blazing fire. My boots and socks stood at attention on spits of wood to dry from the sweat and snow of the day. I wiggled my toes and sang to myself.

> *My Uncle Bill's a fireman*
> *Cause he puts out fires.*
> *One day he went to a fire,*
> *Cause he puts out fires.*
> *The fire it lit some dynamite,*
> *Blew poor Bill clear out of site.*
> *But where he goes he'll be alright,*
> *Cause he puts out fires!*

For a moment I forgot that I was all alone, surrounded by a vast wilderness, and gnawing on a leg of leftover rabbit. Then a wolf howled its lonely cry from the other side of the meadow and I began to cry. *O God, please help me. Please send someone to find me. Please.*

"*Kroo, krooo. Whar, whar, whar.*" Owl danced on the beam of the lean-to. "*Ke-yah, key-yah, key-ya.*"

"Are you the answer to my prayer, little buddy?"

"Ank, ank, ank." Then he launched into the dark. Time for his nightly hunt. *"Whooo-whoo-whooo. Whoo-cooks-for-yooo?"*

T.D. Roth

CHAPTER 6

WINTER MOUNTAIN mornings slowly seep through the darkness and cold. There is no warmth in the early sun. My sleeping bag was so warm. *Maybe just a few more minutes.... The fire! Gotta get up!* Only a few dying embers remained, but that was enough. Soon flames blazed through the receding darkness.

The soft flap of wings and an *"ank, ank, ank"* announced Owl's return as he circled the camp, dropped something at my feet, and landed on a nearby limb. "*Ank, ank, ank.*" His head swiveled left, then right, then back to me. He blinked his large round eyes and stared at the offering he'd brought.

"A rat!? Sorry little friend, I just can't..."

"*Ank, ank, ank.*" Owl did his little dance and dropped onto his prey. Taking hold of the rat's head, he slowly worked it into his mouth and down his gullet–head, front legs, body, and bum.

"Eww! That's disgusting. How can you do that?"

Owl stared at me with the rat's tail hanging from his mouth. He winked one eye, struggled through three hops to get back into the air, and then settled on the peak of the lean-to. I pulled out a chunk of dried salmon. Now there was only one piece left. Maybe I'd get the chance to shoot a rabbit or a grouse. On second thought, maybe not. I couldn't waste .30-30 shells on small animals. The bullets were needed for a deer or a moose. Time to pack and hope that Owl could fly with the extra weight of the rat in his stomach.

He led me to a well-used game trail. The odd deer track crossed the path. I recognized moose droppings. They look like chocolate covered peanuts but "no thanks." A pile of bear scat surprised me. Weren't bears supposed to be sleeping in their dens? The occasional wild rosebush, denuded of its leaves, exposed a rash of rosehips. I picked a pocketful to chew on. They aren't as tasty as they look, and the seeds make them almost impossible to swallow. I sucked out whatever goodness I could. They're supposed to be a good source of vitamin C. The trees became more sparce as the trail turned up the mountain. Water gurgled down a rocky stream bed, forming icicles that shimmered in blue, white, and rose as it cascaded over the rocks. A fools hen eyed me from beside the path. I gave a pathetic try at hitting it with a snowball. The grouse burst into flight and disappeared into the brush. *Drat!* A few minutes later Owl swooped through the trees and dropped it at my feet. "How do you do that?"

The trail crested a small rise and there, snuggled against a rock face, was Chief Jesse's cabin. According to Tommy, the Old Ones had built it when the beaver, otter, and mink were still plentiful. Beaver pelts were traded for kettles, cloth, salt and sugar, hatchets and even rifles. Those days were long past, but Chief Jesse and his brothers had kept the cabin as a hunting lodge for deer, moose, and woodland caribou. It was barely eight feet high, and the sides were only about twelve feet square, not much bigger than my bedroom at home. Leaves and drifted snow blocked the door. A generous supply of split wood and kindling was stacked along the side. A small window was covered with an animal skin that was stretched so thin that it reminded me of wax paper. I cleaned debris from the front stoop and pushed open the door. Stale musty air billowed out. Inside, it was murky and dark. A mouse scurried across the floor and out a crack in the back wall. I stepped in for a closer look and bumped into a weathered old lantern that hung from the ceiling. A rough-hewn bed and a bunk were built along one wall. Two large logs served as chairs at either end of a small table. Inverted tin bowls and cups were placed before each chair. Spoons and forks stood at attention from a dusty, green-colored mason jar. A stone fireplace squatted along the back wall. A smoke-stained Dutch oven hung above the grate and a porcelain kettle sat on the hearth. A frying pan, wash basin, and various cooking utensils hung on the wall. Gallon jars, partially filled with flour, rice, and beans, occupied the lower shelf of a corner pantry. Upper shelves hosted a small assortment of canned fruit and vegetables. It's the way of the wilderness to leave a cabin partially stocked with food and the door unlocked for strangers.

I leaned the .30-30 in the corner beside the door, placed my pack on the lower bunk, and lit the lamp. The first order of business was a fire, then water from the creek, followed by a steaming cup of tea—with three spoons of sugar from the pantry. There's nothing like cradling a hot cup of tea in your hands on a cold day. While the cabin warmed I stepped outside to enjoy the final ray of sunshine and the first peek of the moon. I might be lost and alone, but I felt that somehow everything would work out. Surely someone would come for me.

"Whar, whar, whar. Ank, ank, ank." Owl peeked from a hole in a tall spruce that stood beside the cabin. *"Ank, ank, ank."*

"Owl," I said. "I didn't believe Chief Jesse when he said I shared your spirit. And I can't say that I understand. Grandmother Dubois taught me that you are known as a guardian, teacher, and leader; that yours is the spirit of wisdom. You are more than that to me. You are my friend."

Owl swiveled his head, blinked his eyes, and leapt from his perch. He swooped in a short circle, brushing my hair as he passed, then glided into the trees. *"Whooo-whoo-whooo. Whoo-cooks-for-yooo? Whooo-whoo-whooo."*

Roasted grouse and canned peas would never taste better than those I had that night. I sat and stared into the fire thinking about the following day. *Maybe I'll go hunting. Maybe I'll make bannock. Maybe...maybe.* My eyes drooped as my weary muscles responded to the warmth of the cabin. I stoked up the fire and spread my sleeping bag on the hard slats of the bed. *Maybe I'll cut soft boughs for the bed. Maybe....*

The fire tapered to a dim flame. Soon ash hid the embers as the cold night stretched its icy fingers around the cabin. I don't know how long I slept, only that I awoke when a sliver of light from the top of the door fell across my face. *Where am I? Right. Gotta get up and tend the fire. Oh, my shoulder and hip. Must get some soft boughs for this bed.*

Once the fire was blazing, I opened the door to light the cabin. The fireplace more than offset the crisp morning air. Snow on the tree branches sparkled silver and blue and red. *Billy, you're gonna make it. Someone will come. You're gonna make it. Okay, let's see what we have to work with.*

I set my pack beside the table and pulled out the contents: a box of .30-30 shells, matches, a compass, a roll of toilet paper–grandmothers think of everything–spare socks and long johns, mittens, one last nugget of salmon, and.... *What's this?* A deerskin bag secured with leather lacing was stuffed in the bottom of the pack. I emptied it piece by piece: a twist of tobacco, a bundle of sage, a cluster of cedar, and a braid of sweetgrass–the four sacred medicines. Turquoise, blue, and pink flickered in the light of the lamp from the polished bowl of an abalone shell. Also included was a wild turkey feather with light brown streaks, a dark band, and a white tip. That Grandmother Dubois! My real grandma would have packed a bible and a rosary.

My stomach rumbled and growled. Time to eat. I mixed some bannock from the flour in my pack. A cup of tea and a large scone-like cake of bread is a good way to start the day. I should have known not to add extra salt to Grandmother Dubois' mix. I managed to choke down a biscuit by dipping it in a sweet cup of tea. Before this, the extent of my cooking experience was adding just the right amount of milk to a bowl of frosted flakes and boiling the water for a box of macaroni and cheese. Oh.... I also know how to spread peanut butter and jam; not much help in a small cabin tucked away in the wilderness. Now I needed meat, and more than the occasional rabbit provided by Owl. My knowledge of the woods was limited to *My Side of the Mountain,* a book I had read about a boy that lived in a hollowed-out tree, and *Sportsman's Digest of Hunting,* a picture handbook which I had in my backpack. I can identify a ponderosa pine but don't ask me the difference between a spruce and a black pine, one of which is supposed to be good for vitamin C. Rosehips would have to do. I've seen drawings of snares for rabbits and squirrels, but.... Well, you get my drift. Looking at *Sportsman's Digest* is not the same as actually seeing someone set a trap. *Tommy, if only you were here. You were going to teach me so many things.*

CHAPTER 7

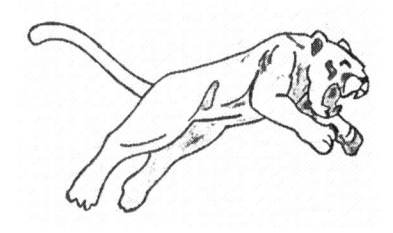

TIME TO EXPLORE. I stoked the fire. Then I placed a cup of dried beans in the Dutch oven, filled it with water, and set it on the grate. That would give them a good boil to start, and as the fire cooled, the beans would simmer. I donned my winter pants and snow parka. An old leather pouch hanging beside the fireplace was perfect for my bullets, snare wire, compass, and a piece of that salt-laden bannock. I stepped outside and strapped on my snowshoes.

"*Ank, ank, ank.*" Owl perched on the edge of his hole and opened his wings in a huge stretch and yawn. Naptime was over. The bird swooped above my head and led the way, gliding from tree to tree down an old hunting trail. He couldn't show me *how* to shoot a deer or set a snare, but Owl could show me *where*. The rest was up to me.

The snow was about eighteen inches deep in the clearings and less than a foot under the trees. I soon learned that the reason a trapper checks his traps every day is not only to retrieve his catch but also to maintain the trail. Winter has a way of adding more and more snow until March or April. A foot of snow today can be two or three tomorrow. Snowshoes don't do much good in deep soft powder.

The burble and splash of water cascading down a small rockface drew my attention to a deep pool in the creek that ran not far from the cabin. Much of the stream was frozen over, but not here because of the falling water. Someone had felled a lodgepole pine over the pool and attached a rope and bucket for drawing water. It looked like the perfect spot for catching fish. *Thank you, Owl.* I sat on the stump of the pine thinking about deer and rabbits and bears and...beans. *I hope those things don't boil over. Sure wish I had some ketchup and cornbread to go with them. Hmm. Maybe I can make some johnnycake using the frying pan.*

The snap of a twig caught my attention. A little forked-horn buck peeked from the brush near the edge of the water. By the time I untangled my rifle sling and loaded the .30-30, the deer was long gone. *Let that be a lesson, Billy. Darn! I coulda had enough meat to last till someone comes to get me. Darn! Next time I'll be ready.*

Owl landed on a limb above me and gave me a wise wink. He turned his head back and forth. Then he winged downstream several yards and waited in a pine. The trail followed along the creek and was crisscrossed with rabbit tracks. I followed the strange three-toed prints of a grouse through a clump of willows. You may have heard of someone "running around like a chicken with its head cut off." Well a fools hen doesn't do much better with its head attached. It just wanders willy nilly hoping to bump into some juniper berries or low-bush cranberries. Four or five deer had been browsing on the tips of the willows beside the trail. Things looked very promising. *"Kuk, muk, qua. Click, click, click."* A squirrel chattered a warning to its cousins that a stranger was passing through. It moved around the trunk of a spruce staying partially hidden while keeping one eye on me.

Owl led me to a rise where the trail forked. The right track followed the creek. I followed Owl to the left. This trail climbed up and over a rocky ridge and then dropped into a small gorge filled with hillocks and gullies. Owl was leading me in a large circle that would take me back to the cabin. *Very smart. This will be perfect for setting up a trap line. Owl, you're a wise old bird.*

"Dee, dee, dee, dee. Dee, dee, dee." A black-masked chickadee raised the alarm for its banditry of brothers further up the trail. *"Tseet, tseet,"* came a reply from the forest as the flock fled into the trees. The friendly chatter of the neighborhood squirrels ceased. The air was heavy and still. Three deer bolted across the trail and crashed into the brush to my right. A brace of rabbits rushed pell-mell up the path, oblivious to my presence. *"Kee! Keeee!"* Owl screamed from a perch high in a lodgepole pine. He turned his head from side to side, peering through the trees.

I froze in place, feet riveted to the trail. My heart pounded and my breath stopped. *Something's wrong. Something is very wrong!*

WHUMP! A cougar sprung onto the trail ahead of me. *"Hsss."* The cat was as tall in the shoulders as the table in the cabin and as long in body as my bunk. I screamed, "Get out of here! Get out!" as I jacked a shell into the .30-30.

Before I could raise the rifle, the cougar crouched on its haunches and leapt.

"Arrrrh!" A small bear hurtled from the dense growth at my left and slammed mid-air into the large cat. The bear and cougar rolled in the snow and separated. The bruin began bouncing on all fours, circling the cat like a hound cornering a racoon. The cougar screamed, *"EEEAAAAARREIR,"* and charged. Razor-like claws ripped huge chunks of fur from the bear's right foreleg. The bear tumbled and fell. It quickly recovered and warily stood its ground. *"Keeeee! Keeee!"* Owl leapt from his perch, circled, and dove, locking his talons deep into the cougar's shoulder. He jabbed again and again with his powerful beak. The cat shook and rolled, but Owl's claws held firm. Then the bear roared and charged. I aimed. *Kablam!* The cougar turned and ran with Owl stuck on its back, struggling to release his talons and wildly flapping his wings.

The bear lay panting in a snowbank. Blood oozed from large slashes in its right leg. Its left ear was torn. It had clearly been no match for the giant cat. Without the bombardment of faithful Owl and the retort of the .30-30 I might not be here to tell this story. The bruin sat up and looked into my eyes as if wanting to speak. Tommy Little Bear's words flashed through my mind. *"We are the Bear Clan. I would never hurt or kill a bear. Who knows, this bear might be my great grandfather come to watch over us."*

"Tommy, is it you? Are you come to help me?"

"Kroo, krooo." Owl wended his way toward us and lit on the ground. *"Ank, ank, ank."* Several wing feathers were in tatters and two tail feathers were missing.

"Owl, thank you."

He did his little dance and blinked both eyes as though to say, "You're welcome."

We began a slow trek back to the cabin. I led, with the bear slowly limping behind. Owl rode on its back like a parrot on the shoulder of a one-legged sailor.

The cabin had cooled from when I'd left. The beans weren't done, so I brought them back to a low boil while I attended to the bear. Several patches of hair were missing. Deep slashes on its leg were full of dirt and bark. I warmed some water and began cleaning the deep cuts.

"Bear," I said. "If you were a dog, a vet would put stitches in these cuts and a cone on your neck. Once I clean and bandage them, you need to leave them alone. Understand?" *Probably not, but we'll hope for the best.* Bear soon stretched out like an old hound beside the fire. He was tuckered out and so was I.

A bowl of beans by themselves just don't cut it. I pan fried the last of Grandmother Dubois' bannock mix. It wasn't exactly like eating beans with cornbread and I missed having a generous squirt of ketchup, but it did the trick. Time to stoke the fire and crawl into my warm sleeping bag. *What a day. Tomorrow I'll work on the trail and begin setting snares. Who knows, maybe I'll get a shot at a deer. I need to get serious about getting some meat.*

I dreamed I was at home eating meatloaf with mashed potatoes and fresh-cooked green beans. In my dream I was only six years old. Mother was tucking me in my warm bed and just about to give me a kiss on the cheek.

"Ahh!" My eyes jerked open. It was pitch black. "Where am I?"

Something soft and wet was bumping my cheek. A horrible smell filled my nose.

"Bear! Aww. Your breath. What do you want?" I crawled out of bed and fumbled with the lantern. Bear was panting. "Are you okay?" He padded to the door and nudged it with his snout. "Too hot? Gotta pee? I wish you could talk. Hold on. Let me get my boots." I opened the door and he limped into the dark and disappeared around the corner of the cabin. I waited for about ten minutes and then went back to bed. *I wonder if I'll ever see him again.*

I was almost asleep when I heard something scratching at the back corner of the cabin. *What the…. Something's digging under the cabin.* Back out of bed. Light the lantern. Load the .30-30. If it had been daylight, I'd have checked it out, but me and the dark don't get along that well. I'd be ready if anything came up through the floor. Whatever it was, it dug…and dug…and dug. I imagined werewolves, sasquatches, and ghouls coming after me. Finally the digging stopped. "*ZZZ – Zzzz – ZZzzz – hng – GGggh. Ppbhww – zZZzzzZZ*" rumbled through the floorboards. Bear had dug a small burrow under the cabin. I would have to get used to the snoring.

CHAPTER 8

I NEEDED TO pack down a base trail and set out snares before the next snow. After a breakfast of leftover bannock soaked in bean broth, I loaded the leather pouch with a roll of snare wire, a half dozen .30-30 shells, a crust of bannock, and a wad of toilet paper. My knife was strapped to my belt along with a small coil of rope and a hatchet. A compass hung from twine around my neck. With all the snow, I probably wouldn't need it. It's easy enough to follow your own tracks.

Bear was snoring away when I left. Owl peeked from his nest, blinked two sleepy eyes, and pulled his head back into the tree. I was on my own. Snowshoeing is easy on an established trail. I took the same route as the day before and soon reached the creek. *I need to make some fishhooks. A nice trout would make a perfect supper. Hmm. What will I use for bait?* Continuing down the path, I was greeted by the chickadee banditos. Mr. Squirrel quickly reminded me that I was trespassing into his territory.

A whiskey jack landed in a tree ahead of me. "*Wha-whi-whit. Wha-whi-whit.*" The name, whiskey jack, comes from the Algonquins. "Wisakedjak" was said to have a mischievous spirit and liked playing tricks on people. They're friendly little camp bandits.

"Sorry, I've got nothing for you, Mr. Trickster. Show me a deer and we'll both be happy."

And there they were, three mule deer munching on low juniper shrubs in a clearing to the left of the trail. I unshouldered the .30-30, gently inserted three bullets through the loading gate, and slowly levered a shell into the magazine. The does drifted into the trees before I could take aim. With the snow cover they were easy to follow. The snowshoes were too awkward for sneaking through the brush, so I slipped them off and stood them in the snow beside the trail. It was slow going. I walked about ten yards, counted to ten, and walked ten yards more. Every so often I saw their little white rumps. They were wary but not afraid and kept moving, nibbling on shrubs as they went.

"Click, click, click...kuk, kuk, muk, qua." A squirrel angrily barked at something behind me. I slowly turned. A spike buck peered at me from behind a small poplar tree. I pulled back the hammer of the rifle and gently brought it to my shoulder. *BLAM!* I missed. The deer turned to run. I quickly jacked a second bullet into the

chamber. *KABLAM!* The deer fell. One more shot and it was mine. I had mixed feelings about shooting the little buck. One minute it had stood alive and curious. The next.... I teared up as I ran my hand down its neck. According to Tommy the animals are our brothers and sisters. Whenever we catch a fish, snare a rabbit, or shoot a bird, that animal gives itself to us. *Thank you, Mr. Deer.*

Once you pull the trigger, the fun ends. How was I going to get the deer back to the cabin? It was only a little guy but so was I. I managed to remove the insides and placed the heart and liver in my pouch. A piece of rope, tied to the animal's neck and looped around my shoulders, provided a harness for pulling it along the trail. It was hard going, and I had to stop many times. It was almost dark when I reached the cabin.

"*Kroo, krooo. Ank, ank, ank.*" Owl greeted me as he emerged from his hollow. He dropped to a limb near the base of the tree, swiveled his head, and blinked at the deer. "*Erk, erk, erk.*"

"I'll take that as a compliment, Owl. Hope you had a good sleep and have a good hunt yourself. And by the way, if you get a rabbit, keep it. I'll be enjoying a thick, juicy venison steak. Mm, mmm. See you tomorrow."

Owl launched from his perch, circled the cabin, and disappeared into the dark. *"Whooo-whoo-whooo. Whoo-cooks-for-yooo?"*

I hung the deer from a beam that was tied between two trees. The skinning could wait. It was time to stoke the fire, brew a cup of tea, and fry a slice of liver. Liver is not my favorite food and is best eaten smothered in onions and drenched in ketchup. A sprinkling of salt would have to do. I hadn't eaten a good feed of meat in days. It tasted much better than I expected. I missed potatoes and gravy. I even missed the vegetables I always tried to get out of back home. And what I would have done for a piece of hot blueberry pie topped with ice cream.

I finished eating and poured a second cup of tea. A fresh log crackled and popped in the fire.

Flames of red, yellow, and orange danced in the darkness. *I hope someone comes soon. What happens when I run out of flour? Do I need to go light on the beans and rice? If I limit the canned fruit and vegetables to a can every third or fourth day there's only enough for a month. Can I live on venison and rabbit?* My eyes began to droop. It had been a long day. Time to turn in.

CHAPTER 9

LIVER AND pan-fried bread are not my first choice for breakfast, but they get you going. I needed to skin and butcher the deer.

The whiskey jack was joyously pecking through a flap of skin and fat as I approached. "*Wha-whit-whit-whit,*" it chattered.

"Out of my way, Jack," I said. "There'll be plenty for you when I'm done. I promise."

Working from the neck, I carefully peeled the hide down and off the rear legs. It wasn't perfect. I would be eating the occasional hair, but it was my first time to skin a deer. I was careful not to nick the skin. I might need it later. I deboned most of the meat into small roasts and steaks. Little chunks of meat, like those coming off the ribs, were saved for stews. Preserving the meat was a problem. Some could be smoked and dried using my fireplace. The rest would easily freeze if left outside but what about the wild animals? While enjoying a cup of bean stew, I thought of an answer: An outdoor icebox made with firewood.

I stacked small logs to form a miniature cabin about two feet square with small upright limbs securing the corners. Spruce boughs lined the bottom, and the deer hide covered the inside. A heavy lid of split logs was tied in place on top. *I'm a genius!* For wrapping, I tore pages from my *Sportsman's Digest,* keeping only the articles I needed. The meat might suffer "freezer burn" and gradual drying but the portions would be separate and accessible when needed. I placed a layer of packages on the bottom of my freezer box, covered it with spruce boughs, laid out a second layer, covered it with boughs, and so forth. My last task was to drag the remaining bones into the woods. Wild animals would finish the cleanup.

There's nothing like a thick deer steak on rice, covered with thin venison gravy. This was the best meal I'd had since arriving at the cabin. I felt good about the day's work. I cleaned the dishes and boiled a cup of tea, then sat staring into the fire. If only I had a television or radio. A wolf howling in the distance aroused fear and loneliness. Almost immediately a rustling beneath the back floor of the cabin and Bear's intermittent snoring reminded me that I was not alone.

Tommy, I miss you. This is not the way it was supposed to be. Where are you now? If your great grandfather's spirit was in the bear on the river, is your spirit in the bear beneath the floor? Was it you that saved me from the cougar? Whose spirit is in Owl? I don't understand. What will they think when they find my snowmobile? How long will they keep looking for me? For now I have Owl and Bear. The cabin is warm and snug. And I have food. But will anyone come for me?

One problem that plagued me was how to calculate time. Nature doesn't care about the days of the week. The days seemed to be getting shorter, which meant that December hadn't passed. I etched a mark on the wall every night to keep a rough count, but I'd been at the cabin for a week or so before I started. To make matters worse, I didn't have a watch. Owl alerted me every evening when he began his nightly pursuit of rabbits and again every morning when he returned. But he didn't stick to a strict schedule. Daylight in midwinter is only about eight hours. Take away eight hours for sleep and there are still eight hours to fill either in the dark or with dim lamplight. Not having a watch, I found this baffling. Should I stay awake until I can't hold my eyes open? When I wake up in the dark, is it time to get up?

Now I understand why bears hibernate in the winter.

I finished my tea and brought out the .30-30. There was no telling when it had last been cleaned, and I had plenty of time. I rubbed the stock and barrel with melted venison fat to repel snow and water, making certain not to get any oil into the trigger or magazine. Heavy oil will harden in the cold and jam the action. I pushed a small piece of oily rag through the barrel with a long, skinny willow branch. It came out black with powder residue. I ran two more patches through to ensure that no grease was left. When finished, I levered the action, aimed at a peg in the wall, and squeezed the trigger—a way of practicing without any bullets in the rifle. I learned later that "dry firing" without a dummy bullet in the chamber can sometimes damage the firing pin.

Before propping the rifle back in the corner beside the door, I gave the stock one last polish with a clean rag and wondered what stories the old .30-30 held. *How many deer have you shot? Did you ever shoot a moose or a bear? Where did these scratches come from? What caused this worn spot? If only you could talk.*

It was time to stoke the fire and put out the lamp. Muffled snoring rumbled through the floor. "Good night, Bear. Hope your leg is healing and I see you again before spring."

A soft *"Whooo-whoo-whooo. Whoo-cooks-for-yooo?"* drifted from the pines near the creek. "Good night, Owl. Happy hunting."

CHAPTER 10

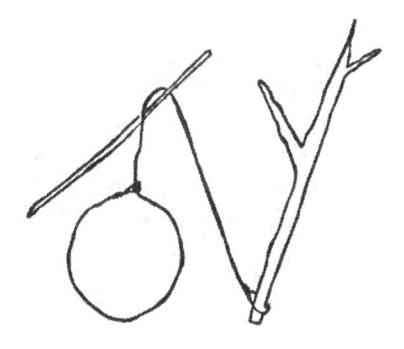

"KROO, KROOO, ank, ank, ank." Owl was home from his nightly foray. Time for me to roll out of bed, have a venison chop and a cup of tea. Today I would break new trail with the snowshoes and set out a few snares. It was important to tromp down a good base before more snow fell. I laid out the equipment for the day: a compass in case I wandered from the trail and needed to cut cross-country; my bowie knife; snare wire; a hatchet; the .30-30; a half dozen bullets; and

several pieces of meat for lunch. Some things went into the leather pouch and others were attached to my belt.

"Huff. Wuff!"

"Bear, is that you?"

"Wuff."

I threw open the door, stepped through, and flung my arms around my furry friend. "Bear, you're back! Are you okay? Let me see that leg." The bandage was gone. Bright scar tissue had formed over the deep claw marks. "You're well. Hurrah!"

Bear gave me, you guessed it, a *bear hug* that knocked me off my feet and into a snowbank.

"I can't breathe," I laughed.

He eased his grip and gave a contented, *"Purrrr."*

"No," I sensed what was coming and struggled to escape. "No," I giggled. "Please, no!"

Slurrrp. His tongue slobbered up my chin, across my lips, and over my nose.

"Oooh! Bear! Your breath! You're killin' me."

"Purrrr."

"Let me get my gear. You're coming with me today."

Ten minutes later Bear bounded ahead like a large black Newfoundland dog. We followed the trail to the creek. *There must be trout in there. And I'll find a way to catch them.* I packed the snow with the snowshoes as we hiked down the path. Soon the cabin was out of sight, and we entered squirrel and rabbit territory. Flocks of chickadees chirped and warbled in the bright winter sunshine. A covey of grouse burst from a clump of low growing junipers. The squirrels loudly scolded Bear. How dare he cross their territory. Didn't he know that he was supposed to be sleeping during these cold winter days?

Coyote tracks and scat littered the trail. Bruins can't see very well, but Bear's nose missed nothing. He lifted his snout and sniffed from side to side, his nostrils twitching at the scent of a coyote that had prowled the trail the night before. *"Grrrr."* He left a large pile of yucky poo; rubbed his back on a nearby pine; then turned around and left bite and scratch marks in the bark. *Coyote take warning, time for you to move out.*

Rabbit tracks crisscrossed the trail wherever we passed through shrubs and thickets. I decided to make several side trails and place snares along the rabbit runs that went from thicket to thicket. I had seen pictures of snares, but this was my first attempt at setting one. I spread my arms to measure out a length of thin wire from one hand to the other. One end was twisted around the base of a small shrub. The other end was looped into a noose a little larger than my fist. The noose was tied with a slip knot that would tighten if an animal went through. Finally I placed the snare about four inches from the ground on a rabbit run. By the end of the afternoon I had broken four side trails and set seven traps–a good day's work. With a little luck

I would have a fresh rabbit stew by the end of the week.

The next morning I could hardly contain myself. Owl had given me a wakeup call and disappeared into his nest. Bear's gentle snoring signified that he was taking a day off. Jack greeted me with a cheery, *"Wha-whi-whit,whit,whit, khaa, aa, khaa, aa."*

I set off, Jack following behind. He greeted the chickadees and argued with the squirrels along the way. Tracks went under my first two snares. I reset them two inches lower. The third snare was missing. A deer print remained in its place. *Lesson to self. Set snares under fallen logs or lean a large limb over them. Deer will step over what rabbits run under.* And so it went. It looked like the day was a bust. I reset snare after snare. Only one to go. *What's this?* A plump little fools hen was tangled in the last trap. The snares worked! It took a few days to learn the proper placement, but the result was a nice plump rabbit every third or fourth day.

T.D. Roth

CHAPTER 11

IT WAS A beautiful day, bright and sunny, without a hint of a breeze. Bear led the way to my trap line but this time he took the fork in the trail going to the right. He looked back at me and tossed his head as though to say, "This way." Within minutes we came upon a small bog. Cattails stood like sentinels along the edges, waving their spiked sausage-shaped heads in the breeze. I watched as the bruin began digging near the open water and ripping plants from the frozen ground. Soon he was chewing contentedly on a mouthful of roots.

"Bear, how did you know what I needed? Did you mean to bring me here?"

I took the hatchet from my belt and hacked through the frozen surface at the edge of the bog. It was hard work, but I soon filled my pouch with nature's "potatoes." I had read that cattail roots are good grilled, baked, or boiled. Dried roots can be ground into flour and baked like bread.

I sat beside Bear and chewed on a piece of venison jerky while he finished his lunch. He purred while I scratched between his ears. "Bear, you're just like a big puppy. Who are you really? Are you Tommy, somehow come to look after me?" He grunted, padded back to the trail, and plodded toward home. I followed, methodically packing the path with my snowshoes.

Bear's rump rolled from side to side as he walked. I smiled. *Here it is, midday, and a night animal, which should be sleeping through the winter, is leading me through the woods. Hmm.*

Owl gave me a *"Kroo, kroo. Ank, ank, ank,"* from his nest as we neared home. He would soon be hunting, guided by the light of the moon. The aroma of venison stew filled the cabin. I had filled the Dutch oven with water, a scoop of beans, and small chunks of deer before leaving that morning. After stoking the fire and bringing the pot to a boil to ensure that everything was well cooked, I settled down to two large servings of delicious soup. At the rate I was eating, I would soon need another deer. *I hope my snares work and that I can catch some fish. Maybe Owl will help me.*

I had several projects on the go. A homemade rack of willow branches leaned against the fireplace for drying thin strips of venison—close enough to dry the meat but far enough not to cook it. An old can placed on the hearth held deer fat. By slowly heating the fat at a low temperature it was melting into tallow for cooking. Tallow can also be made into candles. My supply of beans, rice, and flour were running low and only a half dozen cans of vegetables were left. *Someone better come soon.*

The cattail roots were my project for the evening. I peeled the dark outer layer from the roots and took a bite of the milky white interior. It felt pasty on my tongue. The starch melted in my mouth, leaving chewy fibers which I spat out. Next I boiled a half dozen tubers. The water turned white and slimy like the water from boiled potatoes. Speaking of which, the smell reminded me of potatoes. *Mom, what I wouldn't do to dig into a helping of your mashed potatoes.* The boiled roots tasted like something between carrots and potatoes, quite yummy and much better than the raw tubers.

There are two ways of making cattail flour. One is to place chunks of the inner root in a pan of water and then break them up with your fingers. The starch dissolves and floats to the bottom of the pan. After it has settled, the water is poured off and the powder is allowed to dry into a fine flour. The other way is to break up the chunks over a cutting board and grind the starchy pieces into a coarse flour. Either way entails a lot of work, but the resultant pancakes are yummy.

T.D. Roth

CHAPTER 12

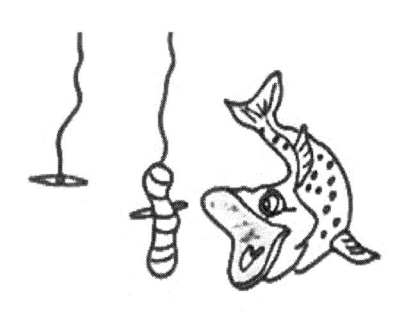

I NEEDED FISHING gear. There was no fishing pole or tackle in the cabin. I didn't have the luxury of safety pins and there was no stiff wire that could be bent into makeshift hooks. But I had abundant wood and my trustworthy bowie knife. Instead of tying two small twigs together in the form of a V with one side tied to the line and the other sharpened into a point, I determined to use just one. Imagine a toothpick with the line tied in the middle. I whittled a short, fat "toothpick" that was thick in the middle so it wouldn't break. A fishing line was then tied to the center. This mini skewer could be inserted into a small piece of liver, a large grub, or other bait. When the bait is seized by an unsuspecting fish, one end or the other will catch inside the fish's mouth. As the fish darts away, the string straightens the "hook" with one point hooking the fish or both points snagging the gills. It's supposed to be a surefire way to catch a trout which has a large mouth and bolts with the bait. I would soon put one to the test.

"KROO, KROO. Ank, ank, ank." Owl signaled his return from a night of hunting. He was ready for a nap and I had things to do. I fried a venison steak and placed thinly cut cattail root into the grease, my own style of "fried potatoes." *Mmm, mm.*

Bear joined me as I trekked to the creek. The splash and gurgle of water tumbling over the rocks beckoned me to the ice-free pool at the base of the boulders. I measured out about ten feet of line and attached a homemade "hook." I used a small wood grub for bait and a few wraps of wire for weight. Carefully stretching out on the log that crossed the creek, I dropped the line into the open water.

Wham! A trout hit so fast and hard that I nearly tumbled off the log. My immediate reaction was to jerk it out of the water. It flew off the hook, was caught midair by Bear, and half eaten before I could catch my balance.

"Bear! What's the deal? Alright, this one is yours, but the rest are mine."

Within minutes four nice trout floundered in a snowbank: one for supper, two for my makeshift freezer, and one to dry beside the fire.

Bear lumbered ahead as we left the creek and followed the trail toward my snares. He occasionally stopped to browse on rosehips. He seemed to have his days and nights mixed up, not to mention that he should have been hibernating. I chewed the odd rosehip and spat out the pulp. There's not a lot of energy in one but every little bit helps. I also picked a few to save for tea. Bear acted like I was just another bruin out for a winter stroll.

"Whar, whar, whar." Owl landed on a deadfall and blinked at me.

"Owl, shouldn't you be sleeping?"

"Ank, ank, ank."

"It's a great morning. You lead the way." Owl leapt from the limb, fanned around my head, and dipped from tree to tree as we followed the trail. Bear went second, nosing through the snow vainly looking for ants or grubs that had long since burrowed deep into the ground. I brought up the rear. Being lost isn't so bad when you have good company.

"Grrr." Bear sniffed the ground, raised his head, and moved his nose in a large arch. *"Grrr."*

"What is it? What do you smell?"

He nosed a fresh pile of wolf scat. "*Grrr.*" Large dog-like tracks led to the first snare. Bloodied snow and tufts of white hair proved that I had set a proper trap, but I wasn't the only one checking for game. Of my other traps, two had been robbed and four sat empty. *Mr. Wolf* had checked them all. What to do? Owl, wise owl that he was, surveyed the situation from the upper branch of a ponderosa pine. He blinked and with a "*Kroo. Ank, ank, ank,*" sprang from his perch and disappeared over the treetops. I collected my snares. No point in trapping dinner for a wolf. As Bear and I retraced our steps, a faint whiff of smoke from the cabin welcomed us. A fresh-killed rabbit lay on the doorstep. "*Whooo-whoo-whooo. Whoo-cooks-for-yooo?*" echoed from the woods. "Owl, you're the best!" I called.

I skinned the rabbit, adding the carcass to my freezer and saved the liver and heart. Liver, despite the taste, is loaded with vitamins and minerals. A full moon lit the night, so after a delicious meal of roasted trout and cattail root, I went out to the woodpile. Cutting logs with a Swede saw and splitting them with an axe had become part of my evening routine. It's great on a clear night and gives me time to think. Wolves were the thought of the night; wolves, and what to do about them.

CHAPTER 13

THE PRESENCE OF the wolf troubled me. There was no point in setting any more snares. My food supply was dwindling, and I couldn't afford to share. What if it was part of a pack? Bear was young and could handle a lone wolf, but he would be no match for three or four. Some rusty old leg traps hung beside the pantry. The largest had wicked-looking iron teeth that would give a deadly bite to even the largest wolf. But what if Bear took to roaming in the night or Owl landed to check the bait? I wouldn't risk hurting my friends.

I crawled into my sleeping bag pondering what to do and soon fell into a deep sleep. Wolves filled my dreams: wolves howling; wolves barking; wolves growling. My eyes opened to the loud bellow and horrifying squeal of Bear. I jumped from the bunk, grabbed the .30-30, and flung open the door. The logs from my outdoor "freezer" were scattered across the snow. Packages of venison and trout littered the ground. Three wolves surrounded and lunged at Bear. The leader turned and snarled at me as I raised the rifle and fired. Howling and barking, it led the pack into the trees. I fired two more fruitless shots.

"Bear! Are you okay? Did you come out to protect my food? You crazy old bear."

I gathered up the pieces of meat as best I could in the dark. One of the trout I had kept from the morning was gone. The other was torn and battered. "Survival" took on a new meaning as I looked at the damage. There would be no more deer, rabbits, or grouse unless I did something about the wolves.

As the sun rose that morning, I fried two venison steaks, one for breakfast and the other to take in my pack. I did likewise with four sticks of cattail root. Opening the cabin door I was met with four inches of fresh snow. Darn! Tracking the pack would be almost impossible. Bear shuffled from behind the cabin and Owl emerged from his tree hollow. Bear led the way, intermittently running his nose through the snow like a hound on the hunt. Owl searched from the air, flying in wide circles. I followed behind.

Bear soon picked up the scent and led us up the mountain behind the cabin. The forest thinned into scattered wind-battered trees and rocky bluffs. We hiked over a ridge and into a protected gully of shrubs and trees.

"KEE! Kee! Kee!" Owl screeched from the sky before landing on a tall pine. *"Keee!"*

"Huff. Grrr." Bear stopped as I slowly moved forward peering intently ahead. Below Owl a mound of loose rock and boulders surrounded the opening to a den. Rabbit fur clung to the brush near the entrance. The backbone and ribs of a small deer stuck out of the snow. *So this is where they hide*. Circling below the den, I hid behind a deadfall where I had a clear shot with the .30-30. Then I waited.

I had forgotten about Bear. Waiting was *not* part of his nature. His nose was working overtime, sniffing and twitching, as he ambled to the mouth of the cave. *"Grrrr! HUFF!"* That's bear language for "Come out, you dirty old so-and-so."

He was quickly answered by a loud "*WOOF!*" and a chorus of "*a-ooooo*" as three wolves bolted from the cave. The first one charged at Bear, rolling the bruin into a snowbank. I fired and hit the second wolf as Bear recovered his footing and locked his powerful jaws on the throat of his attacker. "*SCREECHCH!"* Owl plunged to Bear's aid. The third and largest wolf hesitated at the mouth of the den and then fled into the woods. In less than twenty seconds, all was quiet.

Two out of three wasn't bad. Hopefully the other wolf realized it had outstayed its welcome. I rummaged through my pack and pulled out the venison I had brought for lunch. I cut it into three pieces and gave one to Bear and another to Owl. I no longer thought of them as animals or even pets. We were brothers. After eating, I skinned the two wolves. Then I removed the brains from the skulls. Brains contain tannin which is massaged into hides for tanning. I needed another winter coat and there would be plenty of long winter nights to work the hides.

The trek back to the cabin was easier in that snowshoes work better on a packed trail, but harder because of the heavy hides. Fortunately most of it was downhill. Faint smoke from the chimney welcomed us home. A stew of venison, cattail, and the last tin of vegetables was soon boiling on the fire.

CHAPTER 14

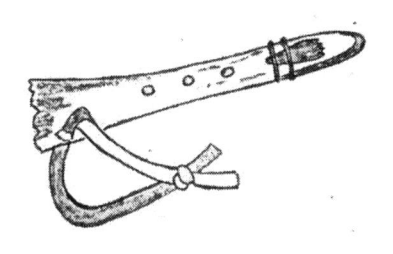

THE NEXT DAY I returned to my hunting trail to reset snares. I set only six in case the wolf hadn't gotten the message to leave my territory. Now I carried the rifle everywhere. With all the shooting I had done, only a few precious bullets remained and each one had to count. Chief Jesse had said, "Little Owl, it takes only one shot. Best to take the whole box of bullets because you don't know which one it will be." I needed more than rabbit and trout to survive. They say fat must be added to lean rabbit meat for your body to benefit. I needed another deer or a moose. On the way back I caught a nice brooky at the creek for supper. I ran a stick up its mouth and roasted it over the fire. No point in dirtying up the frying pan. The night passed quickly. Come morning I ate and hiked to my traps. Though I was by myself, I didn't need Bear or Owl's help to recognize the tracks. Mr. Wolf had followed my trail to every snare and helped himself to two rabbits and one grouse. The wolf was smart. I would have to be smarter.

That evening I sat at the table with the light of the oil lamp. My project was a "dying rabbit" call. A piece of leg bone taken from a deer lay before me. Deer bone, being hollow, can be used for whistles and game calls. I ran a rod through to clean the inside and then slowly carved one end into a slant. A small branch was whittled as a plug for the other end. I used my knife to drill whistle holes. Unlike a normal whistle, this one required a reed. Bone is hard and I worked well into the night. The next morning I went to the woodpile and chose several thin slivers of wood to use as reeds, something like those used on clarinets or saxophones. Back in the cabin I soaked the wood in water to soften it and then carefully shaved it as thin as possible. It took several attempts before finding a piece that didn't split or break. At last I had a reed that could be fitted to the whistle. Testing time.

Quack, quack, quack. Darn! I had a good duck call, but the ducks had long since fled to warmer weather hundreds of miles to the south. The reed was too thick. After another soak, I carefully shaved it thinner. *Kwah, kwah, kwah.* The crows would be impressed. I shaved it thinner. *Wah, wah, waaaa.* Yes!

The next day I had work to do. I packed the rabbit call, fishing line, and a rabbit skin. A hatchet was strapped to my belt along with my bowie knife. Bear emerged from his den and Owl from his hole, and we hiked to the trap line. Fresh tracks showed that Mr. Wolf had already been doing his grocery shopping. Yellow snow at each turn in the trail marked this as *his* territory. A large pile of smelly scat filled with rabbit fur and small bone fragments lay in the middle of the trail like a sign saying, "NO TRESPASSING."

We'll see about that you mangy old thief. This means war!

I chose a small clearing where a clump of wild rose bushes and clusters of last year's raspberry canes protruded from the snow. This would give me a clear shot when the wolf appeared. In the midst of the clearing I draped the rabbit skin over a tangle of rose branches; tied the fishing line to the skin; and then ran the line under a limb below the snow. Next I stretched the string about thirty yards to the edge of the clearing. When I tugged on the line, the rabbit skin bobbed up and down. Perfect! Then I piled brush and limbs to form a blind where I could hide. I positioned an old log for sitting. A large branch lay across the brush as a rest for steadying the rifle. *Every shot had to count!*

There were several hours of daylight left, enough time to return to the cabin for a late lunch. I needed to do something about Bear before taking my post in the blind. It wasn't in Bear's nature to hold still. Even if he could, he would be in the way. I couldn't risk blundering a chance to outfox the wolf. Survival might depend on it. Midafternoon I was packed and ready.

"You stay. Stay!" Bear looked at me and cocked his head. I turned and started down the path. He followed right behind. I turned, "No. You stay. STAY!" He sat on his haunches and crooked his neck. I started to walk, and he bounded up the trail ahead of me. "I didn't want to do this, but you can't come." We returned to the cabin where I took a thick rope and tied one end around Bear's right rear leg and the other around Owl's tree. This was a new experience for the bouncy bruin, an experience he did not like one bit. As I disappeared through the trees I heard a "*Huff! Wuff!*" Then a *"euu, euu, euuuuu"* as he cried like a sick kitten. "You need to grow up," I muttered. Owl came from his hole, blinked his wise dark eyes, and leapt from his perch. "W*har, whar, whar.*"

I settled into the blind about an hour and a half before sunset. Soon the birds would find their perches for the night. Squirrels would snuggle into their tiny dens. Rabbits would poke their heads from their holes, sniff the night air, and hop out in search for bark and buds. Deer would begin their nightly browsing of shrubs and junipers. Owls would cruise the starry sky. Coyotes would run the trails. But wolves would reign. I waited with the rifle cradled across my knees and my hands in my pockets.

When the time was right I pulled the string, making the decoy bob up and down and blew a loud sequence of screams with the call. *Wah, wah, waaaa! WAH! WAAA!* Then a *ma, ma, maamah* like a bunny calling its mother. I kept it up for about half a minute, sometimes loud, sometimes muffled with my hand. I pulled the string and imitated a whimper, *mu, mu, mu, muh,* then gave a death scream with the whistle and stopped as if the rabbit had died. Then I waited. Waiting is the hardest part of hunting, especially when you don't have a watch. I counted the seconds for about five minutes before starting again, mimicking the whimpers, cries, and moans of a wounded rabbit. After a couple minutes, I waited again. A wolf can hear a cry from over six miles away. I already knew that Mr. Wolf had been checking my snares and I was confident that he heard my call, but just how far away was he? And were my calls convincing? I erupted into another frantic, *wah, waH, wAH, WAHHHH!*

I repeated the call, occasionally bobbing the decoy, until it was almost too dark to shoot. Then I saw the glint of an eye as the wolf peeked from the brush on the opposite side of the clearing. He slowly stepped from the trees, warily looking in both directions. *Just a little closer,* I thought. *Just a little closer.* I bobbed the decoy and the wolf bounded into the clearing, moving too fast for a shot. I gave two quick cries, *WAH, WAH.* He stopped and looked directly at me. *KABLAM!*

The moon and stars shone brightly as I skinned the wolf. It must have been the alpha of the pack because it was a monstrous animal. The pelt was large enough for a small cape or blanket. I had a sense of wellbeing as I hiked back to the cabin. That is, until I rounded the last bend in the trail.

"Bear! What have you done?" I'd forgotten all about my furry friend. While I was hiding in a blind, Bear was doing what bear's do best. He'd broken into the frozen food box and helped himself to what was left of my venison. Bits and pieces of meat were strewn on the ground. A couple fish heads gaped at me from the snow. Bear was curled up in a ball taking a nap. I guess bears sleep better on a full stomach. He blinked two bleary eyes at me. "Bear! How could you?"

I untied his leg. He blinked again and ambled to his den beneath the cabin. Soon a contented snore rumbled from the back section of the floor. I had enough food in the house for a couple days but now fishing and hunting were critical. Tomorrow I'd reset the snares, dig roots, and throw a line into the creek. I felt better after a warm bowl of venison stew. I drank a hot cup of cedar tea with an extra spoonful of my diminishing sugar in celebration of bagging the wolf. Looking at the empty pantry, I sighed, "Bears will be bears. What am I going to do with that big lug?"

T.D. Roth

CHAPTER 15

FOOD AND FIRE became an obsession. A rough-hewn bow saw became part of my everyday equipment. It was good for sawing through small deadfalls, and I could carry a six- or eight-foot log on my shoulder. Every day I brought home at least one small log. Nights were for cutting, splitting, and stacking fuel for the fire. I located four places on the stream where the water flowed into small pools. Chopping through the ice was hard work but if done daily I could keep the water open. Baited hooks hung every six inches at various lengths from poles that were laid across the creek. The rabbit snares were checked every day and occasionally moved to new locations. Cattail roots had to be dug, cleaned, and stored. Occasionally I took time to peel the inner bark from the pines. Like cattail roots, the milky-white bark can be dried and ground into flour. I found it easier to cut it into thin noodle-like strips for use in stews. I paid great attention to the squirrels, hoping to find their caches of nuts and dried berries. And I checked the odd pinecone, looking for nuts the squirrels might have missed. The squirrels also became a target for a smaller version of the rabbit snare.

I was losing weight and energy and desperately needed fat. Bear meat was out of the question though I was sorely tempted by Bear's gentle snoring under the cabin. I hadn't seen him since he'd emptied my freezer. Maybe he was sparing me from the temptation of a juicy bear steak. Owl joined me one morning while I followed a new path looking for rosehips. He landed on the outstretched root of a fallen tree. "*Kroo, kroo. Ank, ank, ank.*" Then he took to the air and swooped to a tall pine about forty yards down the trail. "*Ank, ank, ank.*"

"What? Do you want me to follow?"

"*Ock, ock, ock. Buhoo.*"

"Okay. Wait up. I'm coming."

He led me through the trees and over a rise. Squirrels angrily chattered as I entered their neck of the woods. This was further from camp than I liked to hunt. I'm always mindful that I have to hike back to the cabin. When the sun sets, the darkness quickly swallows up the surroundings, and the cold bitterly cuts through boots and mitts. Owl stopped at a rocky outcrop beside a large bramble of roses. Right away I noticed that the tips of the branches had been freshly nibbled and eaten. The jumbled tracks of several deer covered the area and then followed a trail through the trees.

They were back! It was time for some serious hunting.

Since deer come out just before sunset to begin their nightly browse, the timing was perfect. I hid my supplies in a brush pile and climbed a nearby pine tree overlooking the brambles. Deer are creatures of habit and often follow a pattern. Hopefully they would return. I sat with my legs dangling over a limb and my back against the trunk. *What am I doing here? I'm alone; I'm lost; no one has come for me. I don't know whether it's December or January.* I thought about Tommy and Chief Jesse. I wondered how my mom was doing and began to cry. I looked up and prayed, "I need your help. Please give me a sign that I'm not alone. Please."

A small black-capped chickadee fluttered through the pine needles and landed on the barrel of my rifle. "*Chick, chick, chickadee, dee, dee, dee. Chickadee, dee.*" I didn't know if it was telling me off or questioning the sanity of a boy who climbs trees in the middle of the winter. It hopped up the barrel to the sites, cocked its little head, and chirped. *"Chickadee, dee, dee, dee."* The little bird flitted to the trunk of the tree and hung upside down not six inches from my face. *"Feee, bee, bee,"* it sang. *"Fee, bee, bee."*

Thank you, God. Thank you for answering my prayer.

The thud of hooves and snap of a twig scared my little friend. As it darted into the brush, a large white-tailed doe led four deer into the rose brambles and began to feed. A good hunter only takes what he needs and eats what he takes. The rule of thumb is that if choosing from a herd of does, go for the smallest. It will usually be a late born fawn and unlikely to survive the winter. Think of the larger animals as breeding stock for next year's meat. I singled out the smallest deer, took careful aim, and fired. A .30-30 doesn't have much recoil, but it nearly knocked me out of the tree, and I lost sight of the doe. The herd stampeded into the trees as I peered at an empty clearing. Surely I hit it but where had it gone? A buff-colored deer is nearly impossible to find once it blends into the trees or brush. I climbed down the tree and slowly walked to the center of the clearing. *It should be right, right...where!?* I walked back and forth looking for a blood splash or trail. Nothing. I climbed the tree, took a good look at the clearing, and lined up the spot where I had aimed. Back on the ground I slowly walked toward the brambles. A head raised from behind a log. Another shot and I had my deer.

It was dark by the time I had it field dressed. I covered the carcass with brush. I would have to come back in the morning. The deer meant meat for the stomach, tallow for the frying pan, and a fresh hide for tanning.

Back at the cabin I celebrated with a pan of fresh fried liver. Even without the onions and ketchup, it tasted like heaven. Life was good but the night seemed so long. What I would have given for a good book. I looked forward to skinning and butchering the little white tail. There's something gratifying at seeing the fruit of your labor—and even more gratifying in enjoying a thick, juicy venison steak.

T.D. Roth

CHAPTER 16

THE WIND HOWLED through the trees. Two pines snapped and crashed against the side of the cabin. I cracked the door to peek out. A heavy drift of snow cascaded through the opening. The trails had disappeared under the blowing snow. My plans would have to wait. The meat wouldn't spoil in the cold, and coyotes and other predators would be holed up the same as me until the storm passed. A gentle "*zzz, zzz, pfft, pfft, zzz*" came from under the back floor—Bear was safe in his den. Owl would be tucked snuggly in his hollow tree. I crawled back into my warm sleeping bag.

The clatter of shingles woke me. Trees in the surrounding woods groaned and moaned in the wind. Owl had given no wakeup call. There was no dim light of dawn through the cracks in the door. Only the faint glow of dying coals in the fire signaled the approach of morning. When I opened the door to take a look, the wind ripped it from my grip. My hunting bag was blown from the wall and the drying frames were swept onto the hearth. I grabbed the frying pan and frantically shoveled snow away from the doorsill in an effort to close the door. Finally I dropped the pan, planted both feet and with my back against the door, struggled to push it shut. Outside, the drifting snow was slowly burying the cabin.

Two days cooped up isn't bad, at least I think it was two days. I didn't have a watch. But the storm went on and on. The only window was now *below* the snowline. The cabin was slowly becoming encased in ice. It was impossible to get out. The firewood was dwindling. The pantry was thinning. Endless darkness can drive you crazy. I felt like a prisoner in some ancient castle dungeon. The wind wailed and the roof moaned. For some reason I took comfort knowing that Bear was sleeping under the rear corner of the cabin. Then his snore ceased and I felt totally alone.

Shelter, water, and food are the survival basics. The cabin provided shelter but would become a deep freeze when the wood ran out. I burned as little as possible, enough to keep from freezing but not enough for warmth. When the firewood ran out, I burned the wood box. The pantry shelves were next. I split and burned one seating log, then the other. The table came next, then my bunk. I couldn't bring myself to lay on the cold, damp floor, so I spread the spruce boughs I had used as a mattress on the floor near the fireplace. Meanwhile, the storm raged on.

I ate every last pinch of food. Even old cans were rinsed and licked. Deer bones were boiled and reboiled, chewed and sucked. My last effort was a piece of deer hide I'd been saving for tanning. I soaked and wrung it and soaked and twisted. Precious calories were burned as I scraped away the hair. Rawhide can be cut into noodle-like strips and boiled. It's not tasty and is swallowed mostly in small tough little chunks. If a rawhide chew was good enough for a dog, it was good enough for me. But it was not enough. I grew weaker and weaker and slept more and more.

When the wind stopped, the silence scared me more than the din and wail of the storm. I was sitting in a snow-encased tomb. If I could get out, the odds of finding food would be slim and there would be no shelter. I rummaged through my pack: three .30-30 bullets, my bowie knife, some tattered pages of *Sportsman's Digest,* and Grandmother Dubois' medicine bag.

I poured the contents of the medicine bag onto the hearth and stared at the abalone shell. I hadn't taken Grandmother Dubois' teaching about smudging very seriously but if ever I needed help.... Well, what did I have to lose? She had taught that you always think about why you are doing a smudge before beginning; that the feather points to the Creator above; and the sage to Mother Earth below. A proper smudge changes and strengthens the person within us.

I brewed a strong cup of tea with the cedar from the medicine bag. When I finished the tea, I lit a bundle of sage and gently fanned it with the feather. This had been my home and I was grateful. I placed the sage in the abalone shell, and using both hands, drew smoke over my head. "O God," I prayed. "Please give me calm and peaceful thoughts. Help me not to be afraid." I drew smoke over my eyes, "Help me see why I am here." Waving smoke past my ears, I said, "Let me hear...."

"Wuff! Grrr. Wuff!" There was loud growling at the door, then scratching and tearing at the wood.

"Bear? Is that you?"

"Wuff!"

I flung the door open and a large black ball of fur rolled onto the floor followed by a small avalanche of snow and ice. I dove on him and wrapped my arms around his neck. "Bear! Where were you?"

"Little Owl?" A voice echoed through a snow tunnel leading to the surface.

"Chief Jesse? You came for me?" I began sobbing. "You came for me!"

"Tommy! Bring the snow shovel and my pack. Quick! Little Owl is alive." Within minutes Tommy and the chief dug their way into the cabin. I laughed and I cried. Was I dreaming?

"Tommy! You're alive! I thought you were dead."

"And I thought you were taken by the wild animals." Tommy gave me his *Little Bear* hug. But you are here.

"How did you find me?" I said. "I thought no one would come."

Chief Jesse interrupted, "First we need wood for the fire and food for your belly. Come. Sit on the hearth."

Within an hour the fire blazed. It was so good to be warm. I stuffed myself with rich venison bannock and washed it down with a large cup of rosehip tea thickened with sugar.

"We thought you had perished," said the chief. "After the avalanche we found Tommy. He was only partly buried in the snow and had dug himself out. He thought you had been buried alive. We searched and searched. After ten days a hunter came across your snowmobile. Wolves had torn the leather seats. Tracks were everywhere. There was no way you could have survived. I thought the animals had taken you.

"Then this storm covered the whole land. It is the worst since *my* grandfather's time. As it passed, this bear was seen in our yard. We tried to run it off by banging pots and pans and shouting. Then Jasper refused to chase it and shared his food with the bear, something a dog would never do. When a small owl lit on our porch railing and refused to leave, Grandmother Dubois insisted that the bear and owl were sent from you to say goodbye. But then the owl flew to the trees, cried as though calling to its nestlings, and returned to the porch again and again. The bear followed the owl back and forth. It was a *sign* that I should follow. But you, how did you come to be here? How did you find your way?"

I told Chief Jesse how Owl had led me through the forest and how Bear had protected and helped me. I had so much to say but kept nodding off.

He gently laid me down and covered me with a blanket. "Now you must sleep, Little Owl. We have far to go, and you will need your strength."

Within minutes I drifted into a deep sleep. I dreamed that I was surrounded by wolves. Bear suddenly appeared to drive them away. Then I saw myself by the lean-to in the wilderness, warming my hands by the fire. Like magic, Owl soared from the trees and dropped a rabbit at my feet. I felt warm and full and safe....

"Wake up." Tommy gently shook my shoulder. "We must leave while there is light."

I had little to pack: sleeping bag, rifle, medicine bag, knife, and snowshoes. I pocketed my dying rabbit call. A last look around the cabin revealed a cold, empty room with a few pots and pans and an empty lantern. Everything else had gone into the fire. It was time to say goodbye to Bear and Owl. I went to the rear of the cabin. *What the...?* There was no den; no evidence of a burrow under the floor; and no tracks. *But, but....*

I walked to Owl's tree. "Owl, where is Bear? Owl...?" The spruce was there but there was no hollow; no droppings or feathers on the ground; no sign whatsoever.

I straddled the snowmobile behind Chief Jesse. "I don't understand. They *were* here. You saw them. I don't understand."

"You will," he said. "You will."

T.D. Roth

Whooo-whoo-whooo.

Whoo-cooks-for-yooo

T.D. Roth

About the Author

T.D. Roth has loved the wilderness from the time he first camped on a trout stream with his father in the mountains of Idaho in 1956. Fishing, hunting, and the wilderness have fascinated him ever since. He currently lives in Kamloops, British Columbia where, along with his outdoor hobbies, he pursues his writing, acting, and music. Other books by Roth available at Amazon:

The Peasant's Gold
The story of Peter Wing, North America's First Chinese Mayor

As the Windmill Turns,
The Memories of Wanda Lorene Baker

The Stories of My Father

The Seagull

From Grandpa With Love
The Adventures, Stories, and Yarns of a Lifelong Hunter and Fisherman

Horses, Ghosts, and Cowboys
Three Novelettes of Western Action and Intrigue.

Manufactured by Amazon.ca
Bolton, ON